FOR PATRICK, HAPPY BIRTHDAY!

Christmas Feet *2010*

A Gift for Carlos

Written by Maureen Sullivan   Illustrated by Alison Josephs

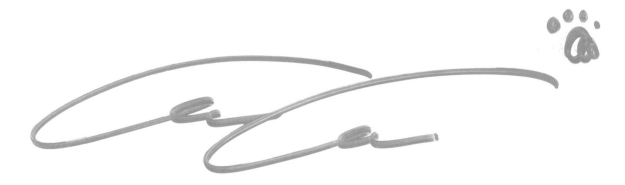

MoJo InkWorks

MoJo InkWorks.

MoJo InkWorks is a children's press.

Text copyright © 2010 by Maureen Sullivan

Illustrations copyright © 2010 by Alison Josephs

Printed in the U.S.A.

Carlos Gets Around™ is a trademark of MoJo InkWorks.

MTA® Metropolitan Transportation Authority. Used with permission.

New York Rangers name and logo are registered trademarks of the NHL team. Used with permission. All rights reserved.

For information contact:
Maureen Sullivan, MoJo InkWorks,
16 Foxglove Row, Riverhead, NY 11901-1216
Phone: 516-695-6690
www.christmasfeet.com   www.mojoinkworks.com

Library of Congress Control Number: 2010910708
Sullivan, Maureen. ISBN 978-0-9820381-2-3. First Edition.

For my darling grandchildren,
Jack, Connor, Luke, Finn, Meggie, and Harrison.
He sees you when you're sleeping, so go to bed now.

Moby

· ·

For G.

A

I had just settled in
for a short winter's nap…
"We still need some gifts,
and some fancy gift wrap.
We're meeting some friends
at the rink 'neath the tree.
Carlos go get your boots.
You're coming with me!"

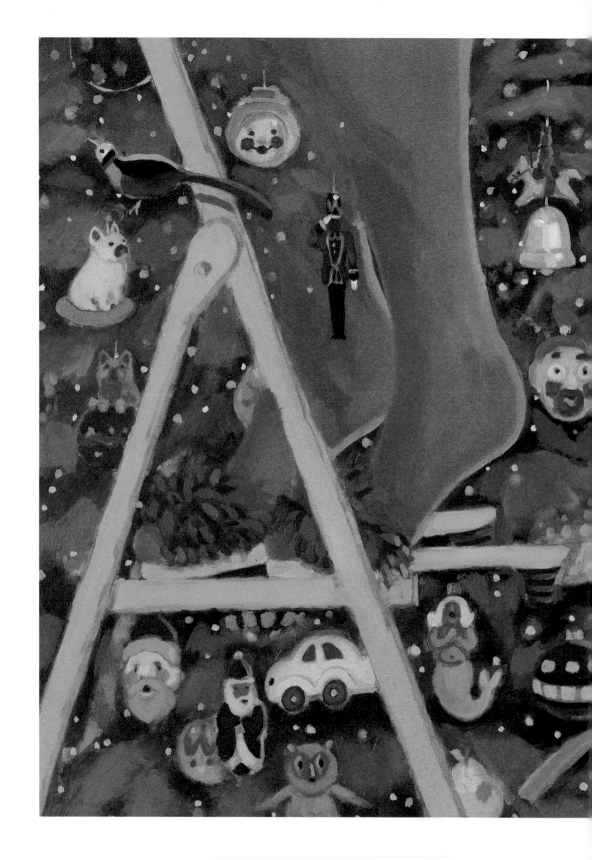

The cab Tara hailed
had no sides and no top.
Its engine was turbo,
his hair a red mop.
"Forty-first Street and Fifth, please,
where the Library stores
great knowledge and wisdom
behind its great doors."

These virtuous bookends,
our city's twin pride,
never let down their guard
over books tucked inside.
They never take breaks,
blink an eye, crack a smile.
They're serious cats
like the sphinx on the Nile.

Behind the Library,
the treasured landmark,
stands a park in the city,
a city in the park!
Where pros perform lutzes
and children carve eights,
while dodging the klutzes
and chaps on first dates.

Synchronized skaters
were keeping the beat,
as I rounded the park,
holding fast with my feet.
Their legs kicked so high that
their toes cleared their noses.
Those **must** be industrial-
strength panty hoses.

A casbah of kiosks,
a jolly brick road,
an isthmus of Christmas,
a Gotham Silk Road!
Where pilgrims seek treasures,
and Santas help folks.
Children drop boots,
and parents shed coats.

Trudging uptown
we saw angel-shaped cakes.
They looked so delicious
my paws hit the brakes.
A peddler was calling out
"Have a great Christmas!"
while warming his hands
juggling red-hot knishes!

We stopped at Saks window
as day turned to night.
At the corner stood a man
with a leash he held tight.
"Season's Greetings, my dear,
have you something to spare?
We place dogs in homes,
where there's love and there's care."

His puppy looked cold,
and it made me feel sad,
so I gave her my boots,
boots were all that I had.
That spirit called Christmas,
the spirit of caring,
hit me square in the mush
when I saw all the sharing.

That feeling is catching,
but not like a cold,
which can make you all sneezy
and can really get old.
That spirit called Christmas
made me merry, upbeat,
from the tip of my nose
to the soles of my feet.

Back home from our shopping,
our lobby was jammed.
Ladies in ball gowns,
gents looking grand.
Said "hey" to the doormen
with high fives and smiles.
Bestowed Yuletide greetings
over gifts heaped in piles.

We opened the gift
Tara bought at the store.
Two new pairs of boots?
Cause my feet come in four?
"What goes around comes around,"
was all that she said.
What's this? Christmas karma?
The same boots? Green and red?

So the next time we leave,
turn the key in the lock,
I won't pull the leash
after half of one block.
I'll brave the cold weather
on warm Christmas feet,
and spread Christmas spirit
to all that we meet.

Sometimes you think that nobody knows
that you're tired or hungry or cold in the toes.
This gift came with love and here's the best part,
meant to warm up my feet, the boots warmed my heart.

The End

A warm thank you to:

Bryant Park Corporation

Citi

City Harvest

Dean & DeLuca

French Bulldog Rescue Network

The Haydenettes

The Holiday Shops at Bryant Park
and The Pond at Bryant Park
Produced and developed by Upsilon Ventures, LLC

Katz's

The Metropolitan Transit Authority

Nathan's Famous

The New York Public Library

NHL

Saks Fifth Avenue

The Waldorf Astoria

And a very special thanks to:

Jerome Barth, Ignacio Ciocchini and Itai Shoffman

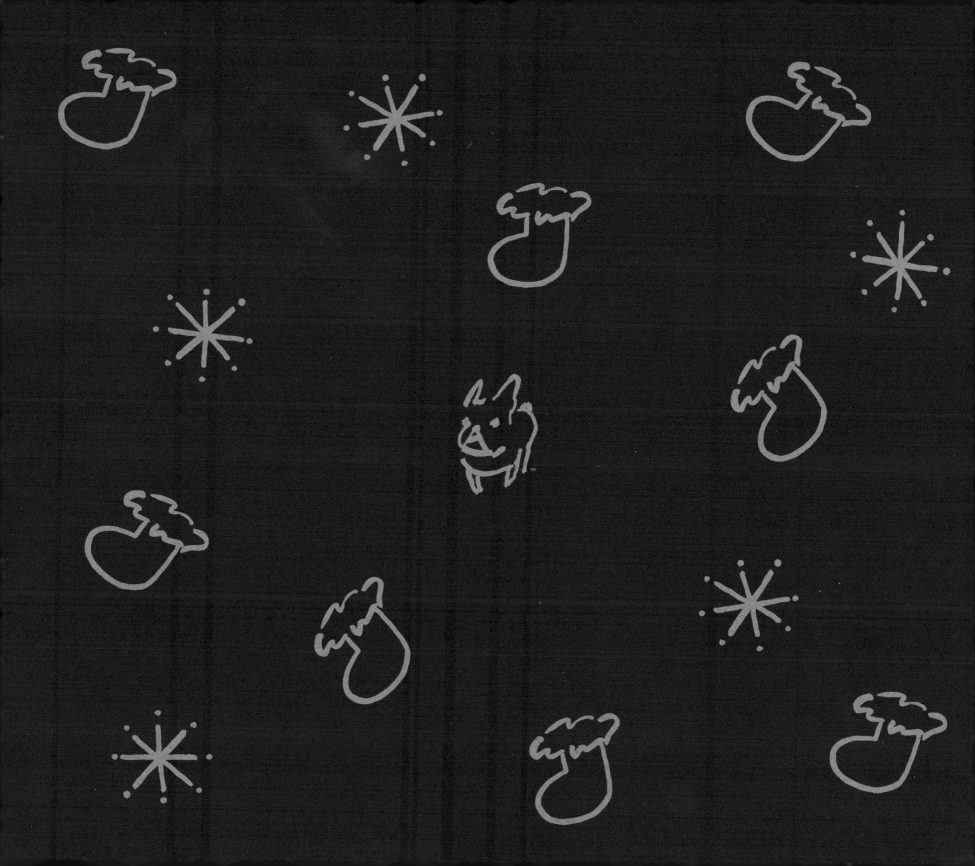